Who's That in My Mirror?

A YOUNG CHRISTIAN BOOK FOR GIRLS

Who's That in My Mirror?

BARBARA DEGROTE-SORENSEN

Augsburg • Minneapolis

WHO'S THAT IN MY MIRROR?
A Young Christian Book for Girls

Photos: CLEO Freelance Photo, 12, 86; Jean–Claude Lejeune, 24; Jeanne Schaitel, 40; Dan LeFebvre, 54; Marilyn Nolt, 74; Michael Tony—TOPIX, 100.

Library of Congress Cataloging-in-Publication Data

DeGrote-Sorensen, Barbara, 1954–
    Who's that in my mirror? / by Barbara DeGrote-Sorensen.
       p.   cm. — (A Young Christian book for girls)
    Summary: A collection of stories about girls who learn that God
loves them just the way they are.
    ISBN 0-8066-2441-8
    1. Children's stories, American. (1. Christian life—Fiction.
2. Short stories.) I. Title.
PZ7.D3645Wh   1990
(Fic)—dc20   89-49097
                                                CIP
                                                AC

The paper used in this publication meets the minimum requirements of American National Standard for Information Sciences—Permanence of Paper for Printed Library Materials, ANSI Z329.48-1984. ∞ ™

Manufactured in the U.S.A.   AF 9-2441

94   93   92   91   2   3   4   5   6   7   8   9   10

For my goddaughters:
Ann Kathleen Collins
Jennifer Joan DeGrote
Stefanie Lyn Olson
Julia Sinclair Snider

Contents

About This Book

Do you ever look in the mirror and wonder who you see? You may have noticed a lot of changes in yourself recently. Not only in the way you look but in the way you feel and even in the way you act.

If you are reading this book you're probably going through a lot of these changes now. Some of these changes are physical. But a lot of them are changes that happen on the inside. It's a very exciting time. It can also be quite confusing.

It helps to know that you and your friends are all growing through this time together. And just like the girls in this book, you all have something in common. You are all becoming the persons God intended you to be.

Sometimes all the mixed-up feelings and uncertainties don't feel very godly. They are. God intended for this part of your life, as uncomfortable as it sometimes gets, to bring about a necessary change in you.

God intended for you to grow up, and isn't that what you've been waiting for?

Think of yourself as a butterfly not quite yet out of the cocoon. It takes a lot of wiggling and squirming before the butterfly can unfold its wings; but the butterfly has to struggle or it will never have wings strong enough to fly. See my point?

And you know, it's not all bad. A lot of it is great fun as you watch yourself become independent, confident, and aware of just how precious you really are to those around you.

As you read the stories in this book you will meet some new friends:

- Shauna, who won't let gossip turn her into something she's not;
- Robyn, who wants to stand out in the crowd;
- Chrissie, who tries to act older than she really is;
- Missy, who only likes to win; and
- Angie, who fights too much with her family.

You will meet others who, by sharing their stories, can help you wiggle out of your cocoon and spread those wings.

And when you reach times when you really wonder who you are, times when you feel cut off from your friends and family, times when you think nobody loves you, hear these words: "I have summoned you by name . . . you are precious and honored in my sight," (Isa. 43:1,4).

That's God talking. God already knows who you are. And if God loved you as a child, God will surely love you as you begin to grow up.

About This Book

You can read this book by yourself or share it with a group of your friends in your neighborhood, school, or church. Each story starts with a verse from the Bible especially chosen for that story. As you read, you will see how the girls in each story put that scripture to work in their lives. (God hates to be left out.) You will also find action ideas that give you some pointers on how to really like that person you are becoming. Try them out and come to see yourself as God sees you: precious, priceless, and well worth dying for. And the next time you ask, Who's that in my mirror? may your answer be Jesus—the one who lives and works and shines through you. Continue to reflect his love and keep growing.

I am so excited for you!

A friend,
Barbara DeGrote–Sorensen

"The eye is the lamp of the body. If your eyes are
good, your whole body will be full of light."
—Matthew 6:22

•

*"Tell me one thing about myself that isn't exactly
like everyone else you know."*
—Robyn

Robyn and the Terribly Typical Day

1

It started out as a normal day. Alarm at 7:10 A.M.
Five minutes in the shower. Blow-dry hair. Look for
lost running shoe. Toast for breakfast. Nothing unusual or alarming. Just the typical schedule of a
typical adolescent who attends a typical middle
school.

"Typical!" Robyn Renoski announced to Jeri, her
best friend, as they entered the halls of McKinley
Middle School exactly six and a half minutes before
the bell. "Everything about me is typical, predict-
able, and utterly boring!"

"Well, I wouldn't say that," Jeri responded absentmindedly, looking for her report for Mr. Harrington's history class.

13

"Well, I would," Robyn went on. "Tell me one thing about myself that isn't exactly like everyone else you know."

"You like pickles with peanut butter," Jeri said matter-of-factly.

"Besides that," Robyn said, dismissing her friend's best attempt to make her feel special. "Admit it. You're my best friend. You know me better than anyone. Even you think I'm boring."

"I didn't say that," Jeri said, hating when Robyn put words in her mouth.

"Be still, my heart," Robyn said, almost fainting as she watched Josh Treeton round the corner. "Now there's something definitely not typical."

"You mean 'Tree'?" Jeri paused to stare admiringly. "No, definitely not typical. And definitely not in our league."

"Why not?" Robyn insisted, not taking her eyes off the cutest face in the whole eighth grade. "We just have to get him to notice us."

"Oh, give it up!" Jeri pleaded. "It's impossible. Josh Treeton—really, Robyn."

Josh, or "Tree" as he was called by almost everyone, was by far the tallest boy in the class. Where the sea of heads moving towards class ended, Josh's head was just beginning. And when you're a girl and you're 5'8" and you're in the eighth grade—well, you notice.

Josh's head floated past and out of sight of the pair of eyes that followed him down the hall.

Robyn began to dig in her purse.

"Seventeen—no, eighteen dollars and 42 cents. I need seven dollars," she announced, staring at Jeri.

"Not me!" Jeri laughed, holding her purse against her body. "You still owe me from last week."

"Please, please, please, please," Robyn begged. "I'll pay you back—with interest."

"How much interest?" Jeri began to weaken.

Robyn pounced. "Oh, come on, we're friends. We can work out the details later."

"Never mix friendship and business," Jeri announced, taking seven dollars from her purse. "Let's see. Ten dollars from the movie last week plus another seven . . . add on, let's say, about 10 percent interest. That would be $18.70 payable to me by Friday. Oh, and I should know what I'm investing in. . . ."

"A haircut," Robyn announced, grabbing the seven dollars out of Jeri's hand and heading toward class before Jeri changed her mind.

"A $24 haircut!" Jeri yelled at the retreating figure. "I want my money back!"

"It's not your typical haircut," Robyn paused to reassure her friend. "Tomorrow, Josh Treeton won't be the only head standing out in the crowd."

Robyn's prayer: Dear Jesus, what did you do to get people to notice you? Help me to look great, Lord. It's really important to me. Amen.

2

"This is definitely not Cost Cutters," Robyn mused in approval as she opened the door of Très Elites and the scent of permanents and hair coloring hit her like a wave.

A lady with black spiky hair and too much makeup looked up absentmindedly as Robyn approached the reception desk.

"She probably thinks I'm selling Girl Scout cookies," Robyn groaned inwardly as she tried to put on her best "I'm cool" face.

The lady was unimpressed.

"Robyn Renoski—I have a four o'clock appointment." Robyn's voice quivered nervously as she eyed the lineup of makeovers already in progress.

The receptionist's long fingernail ran down the appointment book and stopped. "That's with Tiffany," she announced. "It'll be a minute." She motioned Robyn to the nearby couches piled high with copies of *Today's Hair Design* and pictures of sultry-faced models peering out from under the latest hair fashions.

"Definitely not typical," Robyn almost laughed at one lopsided, frizzed rendition of Michael somebody's latest creation.

"Find anything you like?" a voice interrupted Robyn's thoughts. "I'm Tiffany. I'll be styling your hair today."

Robyn gulped and put down the magazine as she took the first look at the person who was going to help her get Josh Treeton's attention.

Tiffany was dressed entirely in black, down to her spiked-heel boots. One side of her head was almost shaved while the hair on the other side sprung out about four inches, looking something like a Brillo pad. Tiffany was not your average definition of anything.

"I want a change," Robyn finally managed to sputter out. "Something not so boring."

Tiffany smiled knowingly as she ran her fingers through Robyn's shoulder-length hair.

"Nice hair, but I think we could do something to make you a little more noticeable."

Robyn, clutching the $24 in her pocket, followed obediently—like a lamb being led to its shearing.

Tiffany towel-dried Robyn's hair and threw a bright red, plastic apron over her shoulders. Bringing her face right next to Robyn's, they peered intensely into the mirror together.

"I've got it!" Tiffany announced suddenly. "We'll leave the top long so you can have some volume to play with. You know, lots of mousse—I've got some great colored gel. We'll see . . . and . . . let's buzz the sides, too. You've got great cheekbones. You should show them off. Parts on the wrong side, though, but we can change that. . . ."

"Yeah, long on the top," Robyn agreed, starting to feel a sense of panic. "It's taken me three years to grow out all the ends."

17

"The ends look good," Tiffany responded, lost in her own creative process.

"OK. I'm ready," Tiffany finally announced and Robin watched in horror as six inches of "nice hair with good ends" fell to the floor. It was too late to turn back now.

Robyn shut her eyes, unable to cope with this sudden move into high fashion. And it wasn't until she heard the buzz of the trimmers that she opened her eyes to survey the damage.

Jeri's prayer: Dear God, now I'm $7 poorer and Robyn's getting a $24 haircut. Something doesn't seem quite right about that. Help me get my money back. Amen.

3

"I told her to keep it long," Robyn ranted, pointing to her semi-shaved head. Does this look long? Does it?"

"It's long on the top," Jeri answered calmly. "It just kind of sticks up in the front. Maybe if you washed it," Jeri continued, trying to reassure the half-hysterical Robyn.

"But you can see my ears," Robyn continued to complain.

"I can see your scalp!" Jeri added. "It looks kind of . . . radical!"

"Totally devastating is more like it," Robyn retorted, tying a scarf over her newly remodeled locks.

"Well, it isn't typical," Jeri continued her pep talk. "That's what you wanted, right? Something so Josh Treeton would notice you?"

"Oh, he'll notice all right," Robyn laughed sadly, "and so will the rest of the school. Robyn Renoski, the totally radical freak! How's this hat look?"

"I'd forget the scarf or hat," Jeri responded kindly. "I think it just draws attention to it."

"It's bad, right?" Robyn asked. "Tell me the truth."

"Really?"

"Yes," Robyn demanded. "Is it terrible or isn't it?"

"It's terrible," Jeri said honestly. "I'm sorry."

"Me, too," Robyn groaned, totally devastated.

"And Robyn," Jeri continued. "I'm sorry to say this."

Robin moaned again. "What now?"

"You still owe me $18.70," Jeri announced.

"Radical," Robyn moaned again, "Just totally radical."

Robyn's prayer: Dear God, I blew it. I really blew it. That's what I get for wanting so much attention. Help me, God, not to be so aware of what I look like. Help me be more aware of what kind of person I am. Make me over on the inside, God. Amen.

4

The halls were empty. It was just as she planned. Sneak into Mr. Harrington's class late. Take the test. Get sick and go home. Only a few marginal kids would even notice. As for tomorrow's plan, she'd have to develop some long-term illness. Robyn had read up on hair in the family encyclopedia. It takes one month for hair to grow a half an inch. At that rate she'd have to be out of school for three months before her ears didn't show.

Unlike other teachers, Mr. Harrington kept his desk at the back of the room by the door. Robyn's desk was only two desks over and only Jimmy Hopkins looked up when she slid into her chair, which was good because Jimmy wouldn't have noticed if Robyn had her head on backwards, much less a new haircut.

Robyn hurried through the four-page multiple choice test on the Civil War and quietly returned her test to Mr. Harrington's desk five minutes before the bell.

"Anything wrong, Robyn?" Mr. Harrington asked when Robyn didn't return to her seat.

Robyn cleared her throat. She didn't like lying. Not even to Mr. Harrington.

"I think I need to go home," Robyn whispered. "My head feels funny."

"Headache then," Mr. Harrington diagnosed, writing out the needed pass.

Jeri looked up and winked as Robyn made her getaway. Head down and full speed ahead, Robyn made a mad dash for her locker.

"Hey, Robyn, watch—" an all-too-familiar voice rang out, but not in time to stop Robyn from colliding with "Tree."

Robyn and her books, papers, and other bits of paraphernalia went flying—along with any hope of getting out of school unnoticed.

Robyn looked up, unaware that she had collided with Josh Treeton.

"Gosh, Robyn. I'm sorry." Josh began to gather up her papers. "I didn't have time. . . ."

But Robyn didn't hear the rest of Josh's excuse. She only heard the word *Robyn*.

He knows my name. The only boy in the entire school taller than me knows my name. Robyn smiled as the thought struck home.

Josh helped Robyn up, and when their eyes met they both began to laugh.

Josh had a buzz cut too.

"Très Elites?" Robyn managed to regain her composure enough to make the most of the moment.

"Tiffany?" Josh asked back with the hint of relief. "I was just going to drop in today to get my assignments and then wait a year until it grows out before coming back."

"Me too," Robyn said, holding her head just a little bit higher.

"Maybe with two of us we could start a new fad. You know, like we planned this," Josh continued. "Think we could pull it off?"

22

"Better than missing school for a year," Robyn heard herself say. But all the time she was thinking what nice eyes Josh had. She'd never noticed his eyes before. And he was nice. You know, really nice. Kind of a, well . . . typical guy. *Except for the hair cut,* she reminded herself suddenly.

"OK, so we're on. Like totally rad, right?" Josh waited for Robyn to join in.

"Totally rad," Robyn agreed, matching the swagger Josh had put into his walk. "Two totally typical, radical people who are never going to pull this off," Robyn laughed.

Robyn's prayer: Dear God, changing my hair didn't really change who I was inside. I'm still typical old Robyn waiting for her hair to grow out. Josh doesn't seem to mind. He kind of likes typical. I kind of like him. By the way, God, Jeri still wants her $18.70. Amen.

Action idea: Pay attention to someone who needs it.

"Be imitators of God, therefore, as dearly loved children."
—Ephesians 5:1

•

"Just because they say something doesn't make it true. I know who I am and I'm not going to let a bunch of lies turn me into something I'm not."
—Shauna

Pick a Little, Talk a Little

1

Shauna sat quietly listening to the gossip going on at the end of the table.

"You know Tracy Nicardo. The one that always smells like cigarettes. Well, Heidi said she saw her downtown hanging out with some high school guys. You know, the drug group."

"So she's a druggie. You could just about figure that one out. She's so quiet in class. Probably high on something and the teachers don't even know it."

"Well, if she's doing drugs, so is Allison Tallet. They're always hanging around together."

"That's them over by the water fountain."

"Quit staring."

"I'm not. They probably wouldn't notice even if I was. . . ."

Shauna turned her back to the group and tried to concentrate on her lunch and her best friend, Lori, who was, as usual, rambling on about somebody.

Gossip was running rampant at Marshall Junior High and Shauna, for one, was growing tired of it.

It had started out as kind of a joke, trying to outdo each other with little tidbits about other kids they didn't really know. It had made Shauna feel part of the group.

"Inquiring minds want to know!" they had all chanted at the beginning of the whole mess. It was fun and at least they weren't talking about her. *Lori would have told me if they were,* Shauna thought.

But it had gotten too mean for Shauna to enjoy anymore. Yesterday, Beth had left choir crying. Lori said it was because Lisa had started the rumor that she had shoplifted from one of the stores at the mall. Now none of the kids would talk to her.

"Shhhh," Lori whispered as Shauna crunched her lunch bag into a wad. "I want to hear what they're saying."

"Well, I don't," Shauna snapped. "None of it's true anyway. All it does is hurt people's feelings."

The girls at the other end of the table stopped talking long enough to take in Shauna's little outburst.

Heather shot back first. "So what makes you so perfect? You've done your share of damage. You were the one that said Lisa Banes stuffed her bra. She's been wearing bulky sweaters ever since."

"Yeah," someone laughed. "Did you see her sweat in science? It had to be 80 degrees in there."

Soon the attention was off of Shauna and back on Lisa Banes's bra size.

"Inquiring minds?" Shauna scoffed as she slid her garbage from her tray into the trash can and headed outside. "Come on, Lori. I need some fresh air."

"What's wrong with her?" Lisa whispered to Lori in the wake of the retreating Shauna.

Lori just shrugged her shoulders. "She'll be all right. I'll talk to her," Lori whispered back as she followed her faithful friend into the courtyard.

Shauna's prayer: Dear God, I want to quit talking about people all the time. It's so contagious and it makes me feel sick inside. I'm sorry about Lisa Banes, too, God. Help me know what to do. Amen.

2

"Now look what you've done," Lori scolded when the two friends got out of earshot of the others.

Shauna plopped down under one of the trees lining the sidewalk. "What?" she demanded back. "I finally stood up to Lisa and said what I'm really feeling. I'm sick of this whole thing. It's gotten out of control. Besides, what's wrong with saying something nice about someone for a change?"

Lori tossed a quick look back inside the lunchroom where Lisa, Heather, and the others were still huddled together casting sideways glances at Tracy and Allison.

"Well, I'd try and make up," Lori advised. "They're supposed to be your friends."

"Look at them," Shauna scowled. "Plotting the downfall of somebody else's reputation, I bet."

"Yeah, probably yours," Lori said with a hint of seriousness in her voice.

Shauna stopped to stare at her friend. "And what's that supposed to mean?" she demanded. "Are they talking about me? I have a right to know."

Lori stood up and shifted her books from one hip to the other. "Not yet," she warned the bewildered Shauna. "But they are our friends and I wouldn't go around saying bad things about them. They could turn on you."

"Well, even if they did, I'd still have you, right?" Shauna laughed, trying to change the tone of the conversation.

Lori looked uncomfortable under Shauna's gaze. "Yeah, well, anyways, I gotta go. Call me, OK?" Lori said as she slipped back into the lunchroom.

"Let them talk," Shauna muttered, picking up her books. "I can handle it." But underneath the tough words she wondered if she really could.

Shauna's prayer: Dear God, did you ever have people make up things about you that weren't true just to hurt you? Help me learn that I don't need to knock somebody down just to prove I'm OK. Teach me to be kind. Amen.

3

A piece of folded notebook paper taped to her locker greeted Shauna the next morning as she stopped at her locker before gym class.

Probably a message from Lori, Shauna thought, looking around to see if she could catch her friend.

Opening the paper, Shauna quickly understood the reason for the note. "Shauna Stewart cheats!" the note read.

Well, at least they were nice enough to fold it, Shauna thought as she wadded up the paper and tossed it in the bottom of her locker. *I'll just pretend I never got Lisa's little message.*

But the next morning a similar note awaited Shauna, only this one was printed in big red letters and had already been read by some kids passing by.

Shauna tore the paper from her locker. *Lisa is playing dirty*, Shauna thought. *She knows I'm proud of my grades. And she knows I earn them, too. This isn't fair.*

Similar notes greeted Shauna in math class, English, and even in the cubby in the library she usually used during study hall. By lunchtime Shauna had a large collection of looseleaf notebook paper all written on with red marker, all carrying the same message.

"Cheater," a pimply faced boy sneered at Shauna as Mrs. Rodriguez handed back the tests from the day before. The good score she had studied so hard for only embarrassed her today as she noticed several kids glancing towards her paper.

I didn't cheat, Shauna wanted to stand up and scream at all of them. But she didn't. *I'm not going to give Lisa the satisfaction of watching me squirm,* Shauna thought, ignoring the looks from the kids around her and stuffing her paper into her folder.

Shauna was the last one to join the regular group of girls in the lunchroom that day. Armed with the pile of notes she had collected and a long speech she had prepared for Lisa, she took a deep breath and headed for the table.

"Oh, it's getting around all right," Lori was saying. "I hit every room except the principal's."

"Serves her right. She always thinks she's so much better than anyone else," Heather added.

"This should teach her a lesson!" Lisa laughed. "Nothing's more important to Shauna than her grades."

Shauna felt like she had been punched in the stomach. It wasn't Lisa who had planted all those notes. It was Lori. And Heather and Lisa knew all about it, too.

Shauna put the wadded-up notes on the table. "Don't let me interrupt," she said, looking straight at Lori, "but I believe these belong to you."

Just because they say something doesn't make it true. I know who I am and I'm not going to let a bunch of lies turn me into something I'm not, Shauna told herself as she hurried to the nearest bathroom and barricaded herself behind one of the doors.

31

Shauna's prayer: *Dear God, I know I'm right about the gossiping. Help me be strong. I know this will all work out. Amen.*

4

Shauna slammed the backdoor wanting to pretend the day had never happened and that she and Lori were still friends. But even if she had a hundred doors to slam it wouldn't take away the anger and hurt she felt.

"Lori lied to me and she's probably laughing about it right now," Shauna muttered to herself. "If that's what best friends do, who needs them," Shauna continued as she poured herself an extra big bowl of cereal. Eating always made her feel better. Especially when she was mad.

"What's this?" Shauna's brother, Steve, asked, holding up a familiar piece of notebook paper marked in red. "Shauna cheats? Since when does my sister, the one with all the brains in this family, need to cheat?"

"Where'd you find it?" Shauna demanded, grabbing it out of his hands and launching it toward the garbage.

"On the stairwell by the science room. This wouldn't have anything to do with Lisa Banes's bra size, would it?"

Shauna felt her face grow red. "How did you know about that?" she asked, more than a little embarrassed that her brother knew about her little rumor.

"Word gets around," Steve smiled kindly. "But I guess you already know that. I'd say you're in a little bit of trouble."

Shauna laughed sadly. "If you mean having the whole school think you're a cheater and then finding out it was your best friend who told them . . . yeah, I guess you could say I'm having a little trouble."

Steve flexed his muscles and pounded his fist into his hand a couple of times. "Maybe I can do something about that. Big brother to the rescue or something like that?" he offered, giving Shauna's shoulder a pretend punch.

Shauna sighed and shook her head. "No thanks, big brother. I got myself into this. I can get myself out."

"As you wish," Steve shrugged. "But if you change your mind. . . ." He ended his sentence with two more jabs to his hand and vanished into the kitchen to devour the rest of last night's dessert.

Shauna plopped herself down into the well-worn recliner that was usually reserved for Dad when the dog wasn't sitting in it. Just thinking about the whole day gave her a headache. *Why would Lori turn on me?* she wondered. *And now that she has, what am I going to do about it?*

Lori's prayer: *Dear God, I wish I could say Lisa made me do it, but I can't. It's my fault that everyone thinks Shauna cheats. Help me make it up to her. Amen.*

5

"Notebook paper? Check. Red markers? Check. Masking Tape? Check."

Shauna synchronized her watch with the kitchen clock: 7:45 A.M. If she left now she would have enough time to get to school, put up her signs, and have Lisa's, Lori's, and Heather's lockers waiting for them when they got to school. It was the perfect plan. *And if it fails,* Shauna thought, *well . . . there's always Steve.*

Shauna's footsteps echoed in the almost-deserted hallway. A janitor watched her suspiciously as she knelt by Lori's locker.

"Keep your tape off the paint, OK?" he said, stepping over the papers Shauna had lying on the floor.

"Ah, sure. No problem," Shauna agreed. But her heart was in her throat as she taped the first of her messages on the front of Lori's locker.

Shauna tried to imagine the look on Lori's face. *She'll be able to read that a mile away,* Shauna thought as she picked up her stuff and headed down the hall and around the corner to Lisa's and Heather's lockers.

Bathroom mirrors. Check. Science stairwell. Check. Library cubbies. Check. That's it, I've covered it all. Now to wait for lunch. They'll be speechless for once, Shauna thought gleefully as she tossed the paper, markers, and tape into her locker and gave it a final slam.

Math went fairly quickly and the surprise quiz in English made Shauna almost stop thinking about Lori and the others. The lunch bell was the signal and Shauna nearly flew down the hall to get to their table first.

A completely composed, sweetly smiling Shauna greeted the confused and befuddled trio of Lisa, Heather, and Lori. This was it. The moment of truth.

"What's this supposed to mean?" Lisa demanded as she held up a slightly crumpled piece of notebook paper with Shauna's handwriting all over it.

"Yeah, I don't get it," Heather piped in. "I thought you were mad. I sure would be after what Lori said about you."

"Lori?" Shauna said, loving every minute. "My sweet, wonderful, multi-gifted, not-bad-looking, best friend in the whole world? That Lori?" Shauna paused dramatically to stuff half a hard-boiled egg in her mouth. "I forgive her."

"She's cracked up completely!" Heather said laughingly. "This should be good."

Lori laid Shauna's message on the table. "I don't deserve this: 'Lori Bently is a great friend.' I don't get it. You want me to feel guilty or something? OK. I feel guilty!"

Shauna took a deep breath. "I don't want you to feel guilty. I just want to be friends again. OK?"

Lori stood silent for a full minute before dropping Shauna's message on the table and mumbling something about needing to call home. Shauna caught up with her in the hall.

"Great," Shauna almost shouted at the retreating Lori. "First you try and ruin my reputation and now you walk out on me. If I didn't know better, I'd think you don't like me."

Lori turned around with an odd sort of smile forming on her face. "It's easier to take when you're mad at me," she answered, still not meeting Shauna's gaze. "I'd be mad if I were you."

Shauna breathed a sigh of relief—happy to at least be talking with her old friend. "I was mad at first. Really mad, and I had plans to get back at all of you. Even you," Shauna admitted.

"I wish you had," Lori said, finally looking up. "I would have deserved it. It was a rotten thing to do. I was, well . . . I was scared that if I didn't play along with the others they'd turn on me like they turned on you."

"You sold me out," Shauna said matter-of-factly.

"Yeah. And you forgave me," Lori laughed slightly. "I feel sick."

"Good!" Shauna announced. "That's your punishment."

"Gosh, I feel better already," Lori joked. "You know, I still haven't said I'm sorry. I don't think it counts until I say I'm sorry."

"Well, what are you waiting for?" Shauna almost screamed. "Say it!"

"I'm mortified, humbled, a slithering slime on the far reaches of humanity." Lori paused. "Good enough?"

"Sorry would have been sufficient," Shauna laughed, happily giving her friend a hug. "But I kind of liked the slithering slime part, too."

"You would," Lori laughed full out this time. "You would!"

Shauna's prayer: Dear God, it worked. It really worked. Thanks, God, for the great idea and the courage to carry it out. Amen.

Action idea: Next time you hear gossip at school, do your best not to pass it on.

"There is a time for everything, and a season for every activity."
—Ecclesiastes 3:1

•

"It's time to start acting my age."
—Chrissie

Twelve, Going on Sixteen

1

Christine Tyson slammed her bedroom door so hard that half her homework flew off her desk.

"Christine! Quit slamming that door!" came the instant reply from her mother downstairs. "It won't do you any good. You're still not going!"

It was the same thing over and over.

"Christine, practice your piano," "Christine, get off the phone," "Christine, pick up your room."

"It's my room," "You talk to your friends twice as long as I do," "I never wanted to take piano lessons anyway," were the usual comebacks. But this time Christine could only clench her jaw even more tightly together and give her door another slam.

"Christine! That's enough!" her mother yelled back.

I don't care, Christine told herself as she contemplated a third slam. "I'm the only person in the world whose mother refuses—*refuses!*—to let grow up! It's so humiliating," she hissed. "Little Chrissie baby, cute, little Chrissie baby," Christine taunted herself in the mirror. "It's enough to make you throw up!"

"If you're talking to me, I can't hear you," Mrs. Tyson said calmly as she paused outside Christine's door on her way to the linen closet. "Calm down and maybe we can talk about it, OK?"

Mrs. Tyson always made a point of staying calm and in control no matter how angry Christine got— and Christine could get pretty angry. It made Christine furious.

"What for?" Christine whined through her bedroom door. "You already said no. Never mind that I already told Jana I was coming. You just want me to be embarrassed in front of the most popular girl in our class!"

"We've been through all that," Mrs. Tyson sighed. "Come out when you can act decent."

"You didn't send me to my room. I chose to come here," Christine retorted.

"Have it your way, dear. Supper in 10 minutes," Mrs. Tyson replied calmly.

Christine heard her mother close the linen closet and go back downstairs. "Come out when you can act decent, Christine," she mimicked silently. "I can't win, and worse yet, I still can't go!"

"They're the best!" Christine had argued about the rock group booked into the downtown arena.

41

"Jana's parents are driving. I've already told them I'm coming. You have to let me."

Mrs. Tyson hadn't even thought about it. "No way, Christine. You know the rules. No concerts until you're 15. Especially that group."

"But mother . . . Jana's parents. . . ."

"That's between Jana and her parents. Your mom says no. You shouldn't have said yes before you asked, anyway," Mrs. Tyson had replied with half an eye to Christine and half an eye on the potatoes boiling over.

"I have rights too!" Christine had stormed as she ran up the steps. But inside she knew it was hopeless. Her mother's mind was made up.

Christine scowled, stood up, and begin to pick up her homework.

I'll just stay in here, she thought suddenly. *She can't force me to come out. I'll refuse to eat. I'll flunk school. They'll have to break the door down!* Christine smiled, enjoying her little drama.

"Supper!" Mrs. Tyson yelled and Christine's stomach began to growl.

"I'm coming," Christine called back weakly. "Food. It'll get you every time!"

Christine's prayer: *I'm too mad to pray, God. Amen.*

2

"I guess it's just you and me," Jana reported the next day during study hall. "Sarah's parents said no. Can you imagine being treated like you're 12?"

Christine's stomach turned to jelly. "She *is* 12," Christine reminded Jana. "Her birthday isn't until the end of the month and neither is mine."

"Oh," Jana paused. "I forgot."

Sure you did, Christine thought as she pretended to study Spanish vocabulary.

Jana never let Christine forget that she was already 13 and had been for four months and 21 days.

Jana glanced up at Miss Pritchert, still busy putting grades into her grade book. "Well, you're almost a teenager," Jana said, "and besides, mentally we're all at least 15."

"What do you mean 'mentally'?" Christine asked, suddenly interested.

"Well," Jana replied matter-of-factly. "There's your physical age—how old you are. And there's your mental age—you know, how old you act. How grown up you are. I read about it in Grandma Hibbard's copy of *Modern Maturity*."

"You read *Modern Maturity*?" Christine said, holding back a laugh. No one ever laughed at Jana.

"It's required reading when you're at Grandma's. That's the only magazine she gets," Jana said, setting the record straight. "Someone can be 80 with the mental age of a 40-year-old—"

"And someone can be 12 with the mental age of a 16-year-old," Christine finished.

"At least 16," Jana said, flipping back to her Spanish vocabulary list.

"At least," Christine agreed, quickly.

Her mother had said no concerts until she was 15. *Well, I'm 16 mentally*, Christine thought. *There's no reason I shouldn't be able to go, after all.*

Christine began to feel a little bit better. Maybe there was a way around this, after all.

"Hey, I've got a great idea," Jana said, interrupting Christine's thoughts. "Since Sarah can't go, why don't you stay over at my house that night. That way Mom and Dad don't have to pick you up or drop you off. We could have a lot of fun!"

"Sure," Christine paused, remembering her fight with her mom. "But I'll have to ask first."

The bell rang and both girls collected their stuff and joined the other students all trying to get out the door at the same time.

"Now take those two," Jana said, pointing at two boys pushing toward the front of the line. "Mental age—six and a half. Wouldn't you agree?"

Christine laughed. "More like three," she countered.

"Hey! Watch it!" a girl yelled from the front of the line. One of the boys said something back, to which the girl yelled, "That's disgusting!"

"Definitely three," Jana joked back as they were carried into the hallway with the rest of the crowd.

Christine's prayer: *Dear God, why do parents treat their kids like babies? Mom never lets me decide anything for myself. Whose life is it, anyway? Amen.*

3

"But, Mother . . ." Christine wailed as her second attempt to convince her mom to let her go fizzled.

"You are not 15, mentally or physically," her mother laughed. "But I must admit you get an 'A' for creativity."

"Go ahead. Make fun of me. I won't always live here, you know," Christine reminded her mother.

Mrs. Tyson put down the work she had brought home from her office. "I'm sorry, Christine," she apologized. "I shouldn't laugh. You are grown up in many ways. But the rule still stands. Fifteen birthdays. Are we clear? I have no problem with you staying overnight with Jana, though. I'm sure you girls could find something else just as fun to do."

"But, Mother-r-r-r!" Christine countered. "That's not the point. . . ."

"Now Christine, I've been more—"

"Am I interrupting?" a voice boomed from the kitchen.

"Yes!" both Christine and her mother yelled back in unison.

"Good!"

It was Ryan, Christine's older brother.

Physical age: 17. Mental age? Depended on the day. Today he was acting like a parent.

"Christine wants to go to the concert at the arena this Friday night," Mrs. Tyson said, catching him up on the details.

Ryan took the mixing bowl he used for cereal and put it on the coffee table.

"That's disgusting," Christine said, pointing her finger at the bowl overflowing with Rice Crispies and sugar.

"Really, Ryan!" Mrs. Tyson laughed.

"A man's got to eat," Ryan defended himself as he shoveled two scoops into his mouth. "Anyway, I hope you told her no! That's a pretty rough crowd down there. Especially before they open the gates."

"Jana's parents are driving," Christine began again, hoping to gain her brother's confidence.

"Really, Christine. It's for your own good. Mom's right. You're too young to handle that kind of crowd. Trust me. This is big brother talking," Ryan said with a wink.

"And this is big mama talking," Mrs. Tyson announced. "Ryan, you will remove your trough from the coffee table and take it to the kitchen, and Christine—"

"So the answer is no?" Christine butted in for one last desperate attempt.

"Absolutely!" Her mother and brother stood firm.

Christine turned and walked calmly up the stairs to her room. Once there, she slammed the door with all the strength she could muster.

"Why can't I decide what's good for me?" Christine complained. "I'm going whether they like it or not!"

47

Mrs. Tyson's prayer: *Dear God, I know Christine is disappointed that she can't go to the concert. It would be much easier just to let her go and skip all this fighting, but I can't. Please help her understand that I said no because I love her. Amen.*

4

"This is great!" Jana screamed as the crowd around them grew.

"Yeah, great!" Christine yelled back, trying to act as if she was enjoying herself.

Christine looked around at the people crowded into the lobby waiting for the concert doors to open. They all looked older than 12, that was for sure.

Everyone was holding general tickets. That meant that when the doors opened there would be a mad rush for the front rows.

"Better move over," Jana warned. "We'd stand a better chance if we tried to squeeze in from the side instead of going in with the crowd."

Rock music blared from the speakers as the crowd pressed closer together. Someone blew smoke into Christine's face.

"This place stinks!" Christine complained. "And I'm hot. Isn't there a water fountain or something?"

Jana nodded. "Yeah, but it's way back where we first came in. If you leave you'll never get your spot back. Anyways, they should be opening up soon. The crowd's pretty big tonight."

Christine hadn't liked the fact that she lied to her mom in order to get to the concert. Mrs. Tyson thought Christine was at Jana's house watching videos. She wasn't due home until tomorrow at noon. Christine had talked herself into coming because she was mad, but now that she was actually at the concert, she began to have her doubts.

Mom will never trust me again, Christine thought as she was squeezed further and further into the corner by the left gate. *If she ever finds out, she'll never forgive me.*

"Ouch!" Jana yelled as someone planted their boot across the top of her foot.

"Watch it, kid!" a gruff-voiced guy yelled into Christine's face as he and several others pushed their way in front of them.

Christine grabbed Jana's hand as the concertgoers crowded toward the opening doors.

"Push!" Jana screamed over the blare of the speakers and the yelling crowd. Unable to hang on to Jana's hand, Christine saw the top of her friend's head disappear into the semi-dark auditorium along with her ticket.

"I'll meet you up front!" Jana mouthed over the crowd, forgetting that her purse held the admission stubs.

"No, you won't!" a familiar voice warned Christine.

"Ryan!" A look of relief escaped across Christine's face as she turned and saw her brother's angry expression. Trying to retain some sense of cool, Christine demanded, "Are you checking up on me? What gives you the right to run my life?"

"And what gives you the right to be at a concert you didn't have permission to attend?" Ryan demanded. "You're darn lucky I saw you squished into that corner before you got trampled!"

"I suppose you followed me here!" Christine demanded. "You always . . ."

Ryan's mouth started to tighten the way it always did when he was really mad.

"Listen, you little snot," Ryan managed to spit out. "Look around you. Do you see anyone your age? No. So wise up, will you. This isn't funny. You could have gotten hurt."

A loud semi-explosion erupted from the auditorium. The concert had begun.

"We're going home," Ryan announced firmly.

Christine glared at Ryan and slowly her eyes softened. "Yeah, let's go home. I've got some explaining to do. But what about Jana?"

Ryan rolled his eyes and sighed. "Stay here," he ordered, "and don't talk to anybody."

Six minutes later, Ryan returned with a confused Jana lagging behind.

"What's going on? Your brother said you're going home. I got a great seat. You can't—"

"I lied to my mother," Christine confessed. "I told her we were staying at your house to watch videos. I'm not supposed to be here."

"Whoa," Jana exclaimed. "You are in trouble."

"She's in big trouble," Ryan added, putting his arm around Christine.

"I'm in big, big trouble," Christine laughed sadly. "I guess it's time to start acting my age."

"Now there's a scary thought," Ryan said with a smile. "Come on, I'll drive you guys home."

Christine looked at Jana. "You probably want to stay. It's OK, I'll. . . ."

Jana grinned. "I'm only four months older than you, remember. I don't belong here, either. This place stinks!"

"Four months and 24 days," Christine said. "But I guess it wouldn't hurt to wait a little longer to grow up."

Ryan laughed. "Like about ten years!"

"Ryan!" Christine complained, giving him a punch in the arm. "I'm not a baby!"

"Hey!" Ryan ordered. "This is big brother talking. Now move!"

"Yes, sir!" The two girls grinned as they followed Ryan to his car.

Ryan dropped off Jana and then took the freeway back towards their neighborhood.

"Christine!" Mrs. Tyson looked up from her paper as the two entered. "Is something wrong?"

"Prepare to be grounded," Ryan whispered in Christine's ear. "But don't worry. I'll put in a good word for you."

Christine smiled. "Thanks. I'll need it!" And she began. "Well, you see, it's like this, Mom. . . ."

Christine's prayer: Dear God, well, I'm grounded, all right. Two weeks worth. But that's OK. Mom said she's doing it because she loves me. And she really does, too. And Lord, help me enjoy being 12. At least until the end of the month. Amen.

Action idea: Have you ever lied to someone who loves you? You're probably still feeling a little guilty about it if you have. Go and tell them the truth. You'll feel better even if you do get grounded.

"Not to us, O Lord, not to us but to your name be the glory, because of your love and faithfulness."
—Psalm 115:1

•

"I'm not here to make friends. I'm here to practice. I plan on taking first chair and nobody's going to get in my way."
—Missy's Prayer

The Secondhand Flute

1

"Unpack your stuff by Bunk D. You can choose the upper or lower since your bedmate isn't here yet," the friendly voiced counselor explained. "My name is Sandy and I'll be your cabin's counselor."

With that short introduction Sandy vanished, leaving Missy alone in the bunkhouse that she was to call home for the next two weeks.

"Summer camp," Missy said sarcastically. "What fun!" She began to unpack her things and jumped up to the top bunk marked D2. "At least from here I'll be able to keep an eye on everyone else and maybe they'll leave me alone."

Who's That in My Mirror?

Missy had been to summer camp before. Not this one, though. This was band camp. "Something different," her mom had said, but Missy knew camps were all the same.

Nobody talks to you. Everyone stays with their own friends. I hate it! They're all a bunch of losers, thought Missy. *At least here you have to practice by yourself. Everyone will be doing that.*

Missy laid out her sheets and blankets and carefully lifted her new flute up on the bunk. Opening the latches, she lifted the pieces from the blue velvet lining. It was beautiful and it made Missy sound better than she really was. Or so she thought.

Missy's fingers whirled across the silver keys as she played the first part of the piece she had used at the camp audition. As the last note wavered off into the corners of the room, Missy felt a pair of eyes on her.

"You have a nice vibrato," a girl about Missy's age said, waving her own flute case in the air. "Hi! I'm Tia Brinklet. Tia's short for Cynthia."

Missy quickly hid her flute under her pillow. *She probably thinks I was showing off. I wonder how good she is*, Missy thought.

"Looks like we'll be bunkmates," Tia continued. "I'm glad you like the top bunk. Heights scare me." Tia plopped her own stuff onto the bunk below Missy's and began to stuff her things into the drawers next to the bed. "Mom says it's best to move in right away. That way you don't get so homesick."

"You get homesick?" Missy asked with a bit of superiority in her voice.

"Don't know," Tia said, pausing for a moment to consider the thought. "I've never been to camp before."

Great, Missy moaned inside. *A rookie for a bunkmate. She'll probably talk all the time about her mom and dad and her cute baby brother.* Missy knew the kind. It got obnoxious.

"Glad to see you girls getting acquainted," Sandy said suddenly from the door. "I just happen to have found the rest of your cabin out circling the snack bar."

And with that, two clarinets, one trumpet, a trombone, and two pairs of drum sticks converged on the quiet little cabin.

"A most interesting group," Sandy laughed. "I can't wait to get to know you. Here's a list of practice times. Sign up before supper. And the first rehearsal is at 7:00 tonight. Any questions?"

"What's for supper?" a slightly pudgy girl called from an upper bunk.

"Where are the boys' cabins?" one of the drummers asked.

"Like I said, a most interesting group," Sandy shot back. "Now, listen for the bell, and I'll meet you over at the dining area."

As the screen door slammed, utter chaos broke loose. Instrument cases, shoes, tennis rackets, a vast array of personal items, and lively conversation came spilling out as the cabin settled in and began their two weeks together.

Missy watched from her upper loft.

"Hi! I'm Tia. Short for Cynthia."

"Megan here," a tall blond carrying drumsticks announced as she practiced a cadence on the end of her bunk.

"Just call me Bo and don't ask what it's short for," another called out.

"Hey, has anyone seen my blue makeup case?" the trombonist asked, digging into her duffel bag.

"Makeup?" most of the cabin yelled.

"Well, you haven't seen the bassoon teacher, have you?" she snotted back.

Missy hugged her flute close to her body and rolled over onto her back.

"Homesick?" Tia asked, peering into Missy's face as she balanced on the edge of the bunk.

"No. Just tired," Missy replied, wishing this Pollyanna would mind her own business.

The bell rang for supper just as the trombonist found her eye shadow.

"Well, you've got to be hungry!" Tia announced. "Come on."

Missy slid down to the floor and joined the others. *Doesn't this girl ever give up?*

Missy's prayer: Dear God, I'm not here to make friends. I'm here to take first chair and nobody's going to get in my way. Help me do my best. Amen.

2

Supper was uneventful even though half of Missy's cabin made complete fools of themselves when the bassoon teacher introduced himself. After dinner, Missy wandered around the camp, finding the practice rooms and rehearsal hall, until it was time for the seven o'clock practice.

"We have an outstanding group of musicians here this week," the conductor began, "not only the teachers on staff, but you, the students."

Missy kept blowing air into the mouthpiece of her instrument to keep it warmed up.

"I've heard each of you play during your auditions so I know what we have to work with this year," the conductor continued, glaring at two tuba players who were talking. "We have an especially fine flute section and—"

With that, half the flute players rose and took a deep bow.

The conductor laughed. "And extremely humble, I might add. . . ."

Missy glanced over at Tia, who had opened her case and was holding her mouthpiece in the palm of her hand. Tia's case was not new. Its ragged lining and tarnished locks spoke to that. The instrument was well used.

Secondhand, Missy scoffed. *She should be no problem.* Missy dismissed any fear of competition from Tia.

Rehearsal went well. The conductor was right: There were a lot of good musicians. Music always made Missy feel better and she was in good spirits as she headed back to the cabin by herself.

"Missy! Wait up!" Tia called from behind. "Mr. Roberts wants to talk with all flutists."

"I would like you all to be at rehearsal a half hour early tomorrow," Mr. Roberts said, "so we can begin chairing this section. Nothing to get worried about. Just a few scales and such. Questions? Good." And the conductor strode off towards the faculty cabins.

Missy's stomach began to churn. Auditions of any kind made her nervous.

"I hope I don't get the D scale," Tia's voice intruded. "I always forget that C-sharp!"

"Scales are a cinch," Missy said, trying to sound confident.

"Not for me," Tia retorted. "You must be really good."

Missy just smiled politely.

"I'm going to be good someday, too," Tia continued. "My mom and dad . . ."

Here it comes, thought Missy, *as if I care.*

". . . both teach flute at the university in North Chester. And my grandma was soloist with the Chicago Symphony for years. It's hard to be too good with a family like that, huh?" Tia joked. "Gram said I could use her flute for good luck this week at camp. It's old. But it plays beautifully."

Missy managed a gulp and a small smile so as not to appear too rude. Tia was not just your average junior high flute player. She was, Missy realized, heavy competition.

Reaching the door of the cabin, Tia asked, "Have you signed up for practice times yet?"

Missy looked at the already-full list. Six o'clock in the morning was the only remaining spot. Frantically checking the sheet, Missy grudgingly signed her name. "Figures. Everyone else took the good times," Missy pouted. "This camp isn't any different. In fact, it's worse!"

Tia's prayer: Dear God, thanks for helping Mom and Dad to send me here. I know I'm going to like it here. I'm already making friends, and I'm only a little bit homesick. Amen.

3

Tia and Missy were up before anyone else in their cabin because of the flute auditions. Missy had been awake and out of the cabin even before Sandy's alarm.

"Six o'clock practice slot," Missy muttered on her way back to drop off her practice books. "Well, at least I'm warmed up."

Tia and Missy crossed the courtyard to the practice hall. "Still nervous?" Missy asked, secretly checking out her competition.

"Extremely!" Tia said, unaware she was being sized up. "It's a funny feeling. It's like you want to do something and you don't want to do it all at the same time."

"I want first chair," Missy stated, deciding to be up-front about the whole thing.

Tia smiled slightly. "That's good, I guess. I just want to do my best." Tia paused. "It's always better to compete with yourself than with others."

"Who gave you that piece of advice?" Missy asked. "Sounds boring to me."

"My grandma," Tia replied, switching her flute case to her other hand. "And she's not the least bit boring. Really."

Missy just laughed. "But that's not really winning. Not when someone comes out ahead of you. Don't you like to win? Cream the competition. Beat out the best!"

Tia stopped in mid-stride. "You're serious, aren't you? I don't know. I hadn't really thought about it that way. I guess I've always won anyway so it didn't really matter. I just like to play. It doesn't matter if I win or not."

Missy felt the air go out of her argument. Tia had never lost. Never. Missy's competitive juices began to take on steam. *Well, it's time for Tia to meet her match.*

"Thanks for all of you being so prompt," the conductor welcomed the 12 assembled flutists. "I've decided to feature the flute section this year with a special piece called 'Flute Fantasy.' I'd like all of you to work on the solo parts during your practice time and we'll meet back here Wednesday, same time, to hear what you've got. Questions? Good."

Missy squirmed in her seat. She hated to share the spotlight with anyone, much less 11 other flute players all playing the same part.

"There is a feature section for the first chair flute on page four," Mr. Roberts continued. "We'll be doing the seating in just a minute so whoever gets the honor of first chair also gets the extra work of learning page four. Questions? Good."

Missy looked over at Tia, busily fingering through the new passages. *Practicing already*, Missy snickered. *I bet she was just trying to fake me out with all that 'compete with yourself' talk.*

Mr. Roberts began the auditions for first chair by having everyone play a B-flat concert scale.

"OK. Now one at a time," he said, pointing to the boy at his left. "Good. Very nice. Watch that intonation," Mr. Roberts commented as he went down the line.

Finally it was Missy's turn. Mr. Roberts paused and nodded. "Beautiful vibrato!" Missy's heart beat like she was playing a march instead of a simple scale.

Tia's turn. Missy tried not to act like she cared as Tia adjusted the mouthpiece of her secondhand flute and began. She was good, Missy thought. No, she was more than good: she was excellent. An ugly feeling crept into Missy's stomach and crouched there.

Mr. Roberts stood up on the podium again. "That was all good. You might wonder what I can tell from a scale. Well, I can tell a lot. Pitch, tone, breath control—all that's important. A scale is never just a scale. Remember that. Tia and ah . . . Missy, will you stay after, please? I'll announce the seating arrangement tonight at rehearsal."

The ugly feeling in Missy's stomach crept up into her throat. She and Tia were about to go head-to-head.

Tia wiped out the spit from her instrument as the others left for lessons. "Looks like he liked your tone," Tia said, trying to break the tension she felt from Missy.

"Yours too," Missy responded, feeling the need to say something nice even if she didn't feel like it.

"OK, girls," Mr. Roberts joined them at the stand they were sharing. "I'd like you to try the first part of page four for me. Take it slow. I know you're sight-reading." He nodded at Tia.

Secondhand or not, Tia's flute produced the clearest sound Missy had ever heard. Her vibrato was even and she played the first phrase without breaking for a breath. But there was something else Missy heard. Not the notes. It was as though a wind was blowing through her music, lifting it high and then gently setting it down. Over and over. When she finished, Mr. Roberts was silent. "Thank you, Tia," was all he said and then he nodded to Missy.

Missy played well. She only missed a couple of notes on the faster passage. Her tempo stayed even. Everything was just about perfect, and yet when she finished she knew Tia had beaten her.

"Fine," Mr. Roberts nodded curtly. "You both are very fine players. Tia, I'd like you to work on this passage, and Missy, I'll need you to learn it also as a backup. First and second chair," he said, pointing to first Tia and then Missy.

That ugly something that had settled in Missy's throat fought to come out. Missy thought she was going to be sick. Picking up her case, she mumbled a quick excuse-me and ran for the bathroom.

Inside, she pressed her cheek against the cool, metal door.

"I'm not playing second fiddle to anyone," she muttered through clenched teeth. "Especially Tia."

Missy's prayer: Dear God, whatever Tia has that I don't have, I want it! Amen.

4

Missy managed to make it through the next few days of practice and rehearsal. Tia's solo got better with every rehearsal, and although Missy's teacher insisted she be ready for a backup if one was needed, Missy stubbornly refused to work very hard on the piece.

"Don't just play the notes, Missy. Think the phrase. Let the music play you, huh?" Missy's teacher tried to tease her out of her seriousness.

"I don't like this piece and, besides, I'll never get a chance to play it. Tia's got the solo," Missy stated matter-of-factly.

"You will play it for *me* then," her teacher insisted. "And you will play it beautifully. The beauty of the music comes from your heart. Now once again from the top."

Back at the cabin, Sandy was announcing a challenge from the boys in Cabin 7 just as Missy entered.

"All right, whose idea was this?" Bo interrogated. Cabin 7 contained some of the cutest boys in the camp. "Why would they pay any attention to us?" Bo insisted.

All eyes landed on the trombonist with the perfect makeup.

"Never mind who put them up to it," Sandy continued. "Do we accept or not?"

"What's the challenge?" Megan mumbled through the contraption she had to wear three hours every day to help straighten her teeth.

"Water volleyball," Sandy responded, only to be answered by boos and hisses from the cabin's occupants.

"Rechallenge them," Megan suggested. "Softball, on the lower diamond. Right after lunch."

"You got it," Sandy said, jumping off her bunk to deliver the message. "See you all there. No exceptions or we forfeit. Eight on a team, remember?"

Missy was happy for the chance to get out of the practice room and forget about Tia's solo and the upcoming concert. She had felt angry for so long it was making her sick. Softball was just what she needed.

Eight boys were waiting when Missy and the others got to the diamond. Missy recognized a couple of them from the woodwind section as well as the English-horn player.

"Places!" Sandy yelled, and the game began.

Three straight outs and the girls took the field.

"We should have stayed with water volleyball," Tia whispered to Missy as they ran to take their bases.

The first boy up struck out. Bo was a good pitcher. *Maybe we have a chance*, Missy hoped.

But the second batter hit one deep to the outfield. He made it to first base and ran for second. Missy shouted to the outfielder, "Hurry! Throw it!" But the boy ran past second base just as the ball got to her. Reeling around, there was still time to catch him at third.

Missy drew back to throw the ball to Tia. Later, Missy would wish she could remember exactly what happened at that moment. She threw the ball straight at Tia. She threw it hard. Harder than she normally would. The ball bounced off the top of Tia's glove and hit her in the mouth. Tia fell to the ground, clutching her mouth with her mitt.

"Game called! Injury!" Sandy yelled, rushing with the others to check on Tia.

Missy hung back as the girls crowded around third base. She hadn't meant to hurt Tia. It was just that she had thrown the ball harder than she had to. And now Tia was hurt and it was her fault.

"She's OK, girls. She has a split lip," Sandy called out as she helped Tia to her feet. "But I think she needs to see the nurse."

The girls backed away as Tia and Sandy walked slowly up the hill.

As soon as they were out of earshot, Bo turned on Missy. "You did it on purpose. You didn't have to throw that hard. You meant to hurt her so you could have her solo!"

"Yeah!" Megan added angrily. "You've been jealous of her all week. Everybody knows it. It was a mean thing to do, Missy. Tia was always nice to you even if you weren't!"

"I didn't. . . ." Missy began to defend herself, but the others just turned away and left her alone in the dusty field.

Maybe I did mean to hurt her, Missy thought as the anger and envy she had carried all week began to turn to a deep sadness. *But I never wanted this to happen. Never.*

The Secondhand Flute

Missy's prayer: *Dear God, Tia's fine except for a fat lip. She won't be able to play at the concert, so I guess it's up to me. Funny, now that I finally got the solo I don't really want it. I'd rather have Tia back as a friend. Amen.*

5

Missy had only one rehearsal with the band before the evening's concert. She had heard the hisses some of the kids did when she stepped forward to play the feature section. After rehearsal Missy tried to avoid the other girls from the cabin by staying in her practice room. She had just finished the most difficult section for the third time when someone tapped on the door.

Missy could see two eyes squinting in at her. It was Tia.

"I know it looks funny," Tia said before Missy could open her mouth. "Just don't make me laugh, OK? It only hurts when I laugh."

Missy tried to think of something to say but no words would come. She wanted to defend herself. To tell Tia that it was all an accident. That she hadn't meant to hurt her. But Tia took care of that herself.

Plopping herself down on the piano bench, Tia looked straight at Missy.

"I know what the girls are saying. That you hit me on purpose. That you just wanted my solo." Tia paused. "Well, it's not true. I missed the ball. It came off the top of my glove. If it was anyone's fault it was mine. I've told them to get off your back, too."

Missy could hardly breathe. "I was jealous," she finally blurted out. "But I didn't want your solo bad enough to hurt you. Honest."

Tia smiled and shrugged it off. "Let's forget it, OK? You have more important things to think about. Like tonight's concert. And I have something for you," Tia announced, handing over the slightly battered flute case.

"Your flute! But why?" Missy said.

"Oh, you have to give it back," Tia laughed. "It's the one my grandma used on all her solos. Grandma said it's filled with love."

"I can't," Missy said, handing back the flute to Tia. "I'm not good enough."

"You are," Tia cut in. "And Grandma said you are, too. She heard you at rehearsal."

Missy took the flute and opened up the battered case. "Thanks," she said. "But I'll never sound like you."

"No," Tia said. "You'll sound like you and that's good enough! I'll be praying for you."

The concert hall was full of parents and family all waiting to hear the night's performance.

Before Missy knew it, Mr. Roberts was announcing the "Flute Fantasy" and Missy took her place with the others from her section.

Looking out towards the front row, Missy spotted Tia sitting next to a large lady with jet-black hair and shining, bright eyes. As she watched, the elderly lady leaned over and whispered something to Tia. Tia nodded and pointed toward the stage.

Missy smiled slightly, feeling the smoothness of the flute in her hands, and that night as she played she felt for the first time the wind blowing through her heart as it filled her instrument with sound.

Missy didn't even hear the applause that erupted at the close of the piece. She only saw the grandmother's head nodding in approval and Tia nodding right with her.

"Missy!" Bo whispered from the side stage. "Take a bow!"

Mr. Roberts gestured for Missy to step forward, but as she did she pointed to Tia in the front row.

Taking up her message, the whole band began to applaud wildly and Tia soon stood beside Missy on the stage.

"I told you Grandma's flute was filled with love," Tia whispered into her friend's ear.

"And all the time I thought it was me," Missy teased as she and Tia bowed together.

Missy's prayer: Dear God, if you ever talk to people through music, I think I heard you tonight. Thanks for giving me what Tia had: the gift of love. Amen.

Action idea: Next time you start comparing yourself to others, be it in music, sports, grades, or just sizing people up in the hallway, stop and thank God for creating you just the way you are. And if you must compare yourself to someone, compare yourself to Christ who loved you enough to die for you.

"Do not store up for yourselves treasures on earth, where moth and rust destroy, and where thieves break in and steal."
—Matthew 6:19

•

"I have an image to uphold. You are what you wear. It's a known fact."
—Mai

Mai's New Clothes

1

Mai tried to sneak in the back door and up the stairs before her mother could see. She would have made it, too, if it hadn't been for Skippy, Mai's miniature dachshund, who was sleeping in front of the refrigerator door. Skippy always slept in front of the refrigerator, and Mai's mother swore she was going to hang a sign on him that said "Diet Dog on Duty: BEWARE!"

"Shhh! Skippy! Quiet!" Mai whispered as the little dog barked his greeting. Catching the urgency in Mai's voice, Skippy upped his bark to a howl. "Skippy! Quiet!" Mai pleaded. It was too late.

"Mai? Is that you?" Mrs. Neve called from her downstairs office. "Can you come here, please?"

"Yes, mother," Mai said, stuffing her purchases into the back closet.

Mai left Skippy sniffing at the door where she stashed her purchases and headed down the hall.

"Any luck shopping?" Mrs. Neve asked, looking up from her word processor.

"I know you said to get only what I needed for school . . ." Mai admitted, trying not to look as guilty as she felt.

Mrs. Neve's cheerful face clouded over slightly. "Oh? Well, let me see it then. You didn't need much, you know. Your closet's already full."

A small scratch on the office door interrupted the conversation.

"Skippy needs to go out. Why don't you bring your stuff and show me what you bought, OK?"

Mai opened the office door and gasped as Skippy pranced in dragging her new designer jeans. A look down the hall showed that Skippy had not spent the last few minutes sleeping.

"Skippy, my new jeans!" Mai yelped, grabbing the cuffs from Skippy's mouth. Sensing a fight, Skippy clamped down with his short, little puppy teeth and began to pull. A tug-of-war ensued as Mai pulled and Skippy growled, twisting his head from side to side as he wrestled some imaginary animal to its death.

"Mai!" Mrs. Neve broke in, and Skippy took the moment to escape down the hall with his prize. "You'd better go get him," Mrs. Neve instructed, "because the jeans are going back!"

"Mother," Mai began as Mrs. Neve stepped into the hallway, now littered with Mai's latest purchases, "I can explain!"

Mrs. Neve's voice began calmly, but Mai could hear the little tremor that always meant she was trying to control her temper. "Mai. This is too much. I will meet you in your room in five minutes. I think it's time for a little inventory check."

Mai began to pick up the debris from what had once been four bags of the newest fall fashions. "Might as well get this over with," she mused, beginning to sense defeat.

Mother's inventory checks could be brutal.

Mai's prayer: Dear God, Mom doesn't understand how important clothes are to kids at school. The right clothes mean the right friends. I have to have these things. Amen.

2

Mrs. Neve opened Mai's closet door and sighed. "Really, Mai," she began, "you've got more than enough stuff to take you into the school year. Just look at this jacket. The tags are still on it. And I remember you just had to have it!"

"Jackie Fenering had one just like it and you know Jackie is not one of my favorite people," Mai retorted.

Mrs. Neve continued her search-and-destroy mission.

"One, two, three, four . . . seven! Mai, you already own seven pairs of jeans. Do you really think you need that pair Skippy was chewing on?" she asked, tossing an armful of sweaters next to the jeans.

Mai opened her mouth to answer and then shut it. Her mother was not in the mood for a discussion.

Forty-five minutes later, Mai and her mother sat with their backs up against the side of Mai's bed, surveying the damage.

"Well?" Mrs. Neve said with a raised eyebrow. "Would you like to have me read the list?"

"That won't be necessary," Mai began. It was no use. Her mother was going to read it whether Mai wanted her to or not!

"That makes seven pairs of jeans, fifteen sweaters—really, Mai—an unusual amount of shirts too great to mention, six skirts, four dresses, and enough shoes to open your own store. That does not take into account accessories, which I will only say fell into the excessive range." Mrs. Neve closed her note-book. "I will now hear from the defense."

"I never throw anything away," Mai began hope-fully.

"I can see that!" her mother responded, tossing another pair of shoes from under the bed into the shoe pile.

"I haven't grown in two years," Mai continued.

"Granted," her mother responded, unimpressed.

"I . . . I have an image to uphold!" Mai stated firmly. "You are what you wear. It's a known fact."

"No, Mai," Mrs. Neve said firmly. "You are what you are. Clothes don't determine who you are. Only you can do that." Mrs. Neve turned and looked right into Mai's eyes. "This is sounding like a lecture, Mai, but it's important. I want you to hear me."

"I'm listening," Mai said, not able to meet her mother's gaze. "But what I choose to put on does say something about who I am. Everyone knows exactly what group you belong to by how you dress. It's just different for you."

Mrs. Neve laughed. "Not really. Adults play their games, too. The big house. The expensive car. Sur-rounding ourselves with more than we really need. It's like you said—an image. Imaginary . . . some-thing made up. Take away all the . . . well, frosting, and then see what you've got."

"You mean go naked?" Mai shouted, grabbing the nearest garment and holding it close to her body.

"Good grief, no!" Mrs. Neve laughed again. "Don't be so literal, Mai. Just, well, sort out your stuff. Get it down to what you need. Not so much what you want. OK?"

Mai looked around lovingly at all her possessions. "You mean throw stuff?" she asked hesitantly.

"Some. The rest you can take down to the clothing bank at St. John's Church," Mrs. Neve began. "Now get going. I want half—"

"Half!" Mai whispered weakly.

"Half," Mrs. Neve repeated, "of this stuff gone in less than an hour. And by the way, you can keep the jeans."

Mai's mouth fell open at the unexpected announcement.

"Skippy's already put his mark on them," Mrs. Neve continued. "But that means you get rid of some of the ones you already have—including the ones with the holes. We'll see about the rest of the things when you've finished."

Mai sighed and began picking up pieces of her wardrobe for inspection. At the end of an hour she had successfully managed to create two rather equal-sized piles—one to go back in her closet, the other to follow her down to St. John's the next day.

Casting one hesitant glance at the "give" pile, Mai bent down and retrieved the jeans with the great holes in the knees. "Some things stay with you for life!" she murmured, tossing them into a bottom drawer where even Skippy wouldn't find them.

Mai's prayer: Dear God, I guess I really did need to clean out my closet and stuff. I still have a lot of neat things. They're just not new. I guess that's OK. For now. Amen.

3

"There!" Mai panted, placing the last of the boxes in her mother's trunk. "What do we get for this stuff anyway?"

Mrs. Neve turned the ignition and backed out of the drive. "You mean money?" she asked.

Mai nodded.

"Nothing," Mrs. Neve replied. "But I'm sure your things will be appreciated."

Mai gulped. "When you said 'give,' I didn't think you really meant 'give.' There's a lot of good stuff in there. We should have had a garage sale or something."

"Do you only give away the junk, the stuff you couldn't get any money for? Why should someone want to wear your junk?" Mrs. Neve sounded upset.

Mai and her mom rode in silence the rest of the way to St. John's.

"I'll be back to pick you up in half an hour. Take a look around while you wait, OK?" Mrs. Neve said.

Mai unloaded the boxes from the trunk and carried them in one at a time to the room where several people were mending and ironing other articles that had already been donated.

"Can I help you?" a skinny woman with gray, curly hair asked.

"I brought some boxes of clothes my size," Mai explained, feeling more than a little uncomfortable.

"Thank you. I'm sure we can use them. Set them down over there, please, and I'll write you out a receipt."

The skinny lady handed the slip of paper to Mai. "We're just swamped today," she smiled. "You don't know of any good volunteers, do you?"

"Uh . . . no . . . sorry," stuttered Mai. "Could I look around for a while? My mom isn't coming for another 15 minutes."

"No problem," the skinny lady said. "Hey, Mildred! Think you could show this young lady the store? She's waiting for her mom."

Mai followed Mildred down two flights of stairs to the church basement. Rack after rack lay stretched out like some giant thrift sale. Large homemade signs hung from the fluorescent lights. "Children: infant to 24 months. Women. Men. Girls 7–14." Mai read each sign as she walked the aisles inspecting the merchandise.

Wow! Mai thought. *This sure isn't anything like Goldwater's Department Store. Nothing's priced over a dollar.*

It was crowded, too. Really crowded. Mostly moms with their kids. Mai watched as one mother tried to pick out some things from the rack marked "Toddler boys" while holding a baby in her other arm.

She looks tired, Mai thought as she watched the young mother struggle with a little boy who was not cooperating. *Maybe I should offer to hold her baby?*

81

Who's That in My Mirror?

The little boy let out a shriek and took off under the racks of ladies dresses, past the winter jackets, and through the jeans. Clothes flew in every direction as the little boy ran and his mother chased.

Mai's baby-sitter instincts came alive as she saw the little boy dash behind a shelf full of shoes while his mother frantically looked to find him.

Sneaking up from the other side, Mai grabbed the little boy and lifted him high off the ground. "Gotcha!" she whispered.

For a moment Mai thought he would cry, but his frown suddenly turned the other direction. "Gotcha!" he laughed as Mai carried him to his frantic mother.

Relief washed over the her face when she caught sight of Mai.

"Justin! That was naughty. You stay with Mommy!" Justin's mom reached over to take him from Mai just as her baby burped up all over the shoulder of her dress.

"Yuck!" Justin yelled. "Julie threw up!"

"We're going home," Justin's mother announced, looking more tired than ever.

Mai put the squirming Justin down and reached for the baby. "I'll hold her while you shop. I've done a lot of baby-sitting," Mai offered.

The mother looked at Mai's fashionable clothes and shook her head. "You'll get dirty," she said quietly.

Mai suddenly wished she had on her hole-in-the-knee jeans and a T-shirt. For once, her stylish clothes seemed out of place and inappropriate.

"I don't mind. Really!" Mai said. "You need a break. And I need something to do until my mom comes."

The young mother smiled as Mai took the baby and began to wipe off her face with a diaper the mother handed her.

"Thanks," was all she said, but Mai could see some of the tension leave her face as she concentrated on Justin and a bright red and green plaid shirt that she had found on the rack.

Mai's prayer: Dear God, is it wrong to have so much when others have so little? Teach me to be fair. Amen.

4

In 15 minutes, Justin's mom had managed to select three pairs of shorts, two shirts, a long pair of pants, and a pair of shoes that looked only slightly worn. The little boy proudly lugged the bag as he headed for their car. Mai waved at the trio as she saw her mother's car approaching from the side entrance.

"Do you know them?" Mrs. Neve asked as Mai buckled her seatbelt.

"Not really. I was just baby-sitting while the mom shopped. I think I really helped," Mai said, watching to see if Justin would wave again. He did.

"That was nice," Mrs. Neve responded. "Nothing's harder than shopping for kids when you don't have enough hands."

Mai sat silently thinking of Justin, the baby, and the mother with the tired eyes. She thought of all the money she had spent at Goldwater's yesterday. She thought of her own closet filled with clothes. She thought of all the kids at school trying to dress better than everyone else. It all made her feel a little sick.

"Mom?" Mai finally said. "Do you think I could volunteer at the clothing bank to baby-sit once a week? You know, help watch kids so parents can shop better?"

"Why Mai, I think that's a great idea!" Mrs. Neve responded enthusiastically. "You can call them when you get home and ask. And I'm proud of you for thinking of such a thing."

"I'm proud of me, too," Mai admitted. "And it has nothing to do with how I look either," she added, wiping off some baby spit from her shirt.

Mrs. Neve laughed. "Is this the same Mai that just bought out the store yesterday? Are you feeling all right?"

"Never better," Mai laughed with her mom. "Can we stop for a treat?"

"You are what you eat," her mother warned good-naturedly.

"Frozen yogurt, then? Quick, turn here!" Mai knew her mother's weakness.

"Exactly!" her mom replied, turning into the parking lot.

Mai's prayer: Dear God, I don't need lots of new clothes to feel good about myself. Thanks for letting me help out at the clothing bank. And please bless Justin and his mom. Amen.

Action idea: Sort through your closet. Take the extra things to a local clothing bank. Stay and look around.

"Do not hide your face from me when I am in distress."
—Psalm 102:2

•

"Some things you just have to learn to live with."
—Jessica

Daddy's Little Girl

1

Angela Joy Wang, A.J. to her friends, slumped down in her chair and picked and poked at her broccoli. Angela hated broccoli, teachers who yelled, anyone with rolled up jeans, and, at present, her entire family. It seemed lately that no matter how hard she tried to be nice she spent most of her time fighting with either her parents or her younger brother, Aaron, and most of the time she lost.

"Angela, don't pick at your food," her mother ordered. "And please sit up. I hate it when you slump."

Angela sat up slowly and begin to push her broccoli under the half-eaten slice of bread still lying on her plate. She was learning to pick her fights. Slumping was not worth a major confrontation.

"Angela's hiding her food!" Aaron announced to anyone who cared. "Look under her bread, Mom."

Angela paused to glare at her younger brother. Unsatisfied with the lack of response to his announcement, Aaron tried again.

"I ate my broccoli," he pointed out. "Angela should eat hers. And she's slumping again, Mom. MOM!"

Mr. and Mrs. Wang were deep in a conversation about the month's bank statement. Angela had also learned that bank statement time was not a good time to discuss anything with her parents—especially things like broccoli, slumping, and Aaron's irritating habits.

"Aaron, please!" his dad snapped, not even bothering to glance at either the hidden vegetable or Angela's posture.

Angela smiled snottily at her younger brother. "Here, have some of mine," she whispered, scrapping the remains of that hideous vegetable onto Aaron's mostly cleaned-up plate.

Aaron sat powerless, looking at the pile of vegetables collecting beneath his nose. "Take 'em off!" he demanded. "You already touched 'em. They're gross!"

"Now Aaron, eat your broccoli," his mother admonished as she continued to rectify a $50 overdraft.

Angela hated Aaron most of the time. She hated how he always tried to be perfect, especially when Mom or Dad was watching. Angela wasn't fooled. Underneath that smiling, vegetable-eating little face

88

lay a diabolical, demanding little brat. Angela knew it. And Aaron knew that she knew it. That's why he was always trying to get her in trouble. At the present, however, his plan had backfired, and Angela was in control for once.

Aaron opened his mouth to complain but sensed that his parents would not respond well to whining. It had to look like an accident.

Pretending to reach for another piece of bread, Aaron managed to bump Angela's glass of milk. It went spinning across the table and into the pile of checks Mrs. Wang had arranged on the table.

Everyone but Aaron jumped back from their chairs and began to salvage what they could from the puddles of milk. Aaron took that precise moment of confusion to dump the broccoli back onto the plate of its rightful owner.

"Good grief, Angela. Aren't you a little old to spill your milk?" her dad reprimanded as he shook milk drops off of the rest of his mail.

"And please, dear, finish your broccoli. Aaron ate all of his," her mother added, smiling sweetly at Aaron who was dutifully wiping the spilt milk with his napkin. "Thank you, Aaron dear. That was very helpful," she added.

"He did it on purpose!" Angela screamed. "He's not as perfect as you think, Mother."

At that moment Aaron began to cry. "Tell Angela to quit picking on me," he whined.

"That's enough!" Mr. Wang began. "Now Angela—"

"You always side with Aaron," Angela interrupted. "I never asked to be part of this family and I wish I wasn't. Just leave me alone!" She stormed as she pushed her plate aside and ran into her bedroom.

Mr. Wang put aside his mail and began to clear the table. "Wow! I didn't expect a reaction like that," he said, looking at his wife. "Was I too hard on her about the milk?"

"She just hates broccoli," Aaron stated matter-of-factly. "She'll get over it. She always does."

Angela's prayer: Dear God, sometimes I feel like I don't belong in our family anymore. Where do I belong, God? Amen.

2

"What do you mean you wish you were an orphan?" Jessica asked. "OK—what did Aaron do now?"

Angela scowled. "It's not just Aaron. It's everybody. Criticize, criticize, criticize. Aaron's just the best at it."

"You're not going to run away, are you?" Jessica continued to probe.

"No," Angela said, "I'm not that dumb. I'll live in the house. A person has to eat. I'm just not going to . . . *participate*, until they quit bossing me around. I'm not going to do anything I don't want to do. They can't make me."

Jessica laughed. "Oh yes, they can. Parents have ways, you know."

The streetlight in front of the two girls flashed "don't walk" as Angela checked both ways and bounded into the crosswalk. A woman in a yellow station wagon yelled something out her window as she zoomed by.

"See," Jessica said, pulling her friend out of the street. "What's got into you anyway? I always thought you liked your mom and dad."

Angela launched into a detailed description of the broccoli bash from the night before.

"They're always telling me what to do. And they never forget to tell me when I do it wrong. I don't have any rights and they're always siding with Aaron," Angela lamented.

Jessica shook her head sadly. "Sounds like my house, only my brother's older, not younger. Some things you just have to learn to live with."

"Well, not me!" Angela stated firmly. "From now on I'll be making my own decisions. Taking control of my own life. Cutting my own path."

"Buying your own clothes, paying rent for sleeping in your own bed, cooking your own meals," Jessica continued.

Angela turned and stared at her friend.

"That's going a bit too far, don't you think?" she asked.

"A.J., I hate to tell you this, but it'll never work," Jessica said sadly. "Parents were made to give rules and lay down the law. It's in their nature. 'As long as you're under this roof . . .,' " Jessica lapsed into a rather good impression of her dad when he was mad.

"I still don't have to like it," Angela protested.

"You're not supposed to," Jessica said. "You're a teenager."

"What's that supposed to mean?" Angela asked.

"A.J., you are so naive," Jessica said as she turned toward her street. "Parents don't care if you're 30. They're still your parents and they're only squelching all your independence because they love you. It's a no-win situation. You'll always be Daddy's little girl. They can't help themselves."

"Thanks for the confidence," Angela yelled over her shoulder at the retreating Jessica. And then she added under her breath, "I'm going to need it."

Daddy's Little Girl

Angela's prayer: *Dear God, if I start behaving strangely . . . please don't take it personally, OK? Amen.*

3

"Car's leaving in five minutes," Mr. Wang announced in a voice loud enough to wake the neighbors.

Angela sat piously at her desk, waiting to be discovered. She was not going to church today. She was ready to stand her ground.

"Coming, Angie?" her mother asked, knocking softly at the door as she came in.

"Ah . . . no, Mom. I think I'll stay home today. I've got a lot of schoolwork. You guys go ahead, though," Angie said, exactly the way she had rehearsed it.

"Excuse me?" Mrs. Wang said with a slight scowl starting to form on her forehead.

"It's OK," Angie continued. "I'll be just fine. Don't worry about me. I'll have this report finished by the time you get home," and she flashed her mother one of her most charming smiles.

"Robert!" Mrs. Wang yelled suddenly over her shoulder.

Angela hadn't counted on taking on both of them at once. This wasn't going to be as easy as she had planned.

Angela recited her whole "schoolwork theory" for her father, who, for once, seemed to be taking her seriously.

"What's wrong with Angela?" Aaron asked, peeking his nose in from the hallway. "You sick?"

94

"This is personal, Aaron. Will you please wait downstairs?" Mrs. Wang directed as she shut the door with a click.

Angela saw the look of dismay that crossed Aaron's face as the door shut. *Finally, I'm getting some respect around here,* she thought, returning to the discussion with renewed confidence.

"Angela," Mr. Wang began, "church is very important to our family. It's something we do together. Leaving you home is, well . . . just impossible. As long as you're part of the family, you will go to church."

"But I don't want to go—and you can't make me!" Angela stated, forgetting her pledge to herself that she would not get angry.

"I think we should discuss this when we get home," Mrs. Wang said, looking at her watch.

"Good idea," Mr. Wang agreed. "The car leaves in five minutes and I expect you to be in it, Angela. I'll help you with that report when we get home."

Angela calmly straightened the papers from her report and laid them neatly in a pile, her well-sharpened pencil on top. "I'll come . . . but I won't sing," she mumbled.

"That, my dear, is entirely up to you," her mother conceded good-naturedly.

"Angela: don't leave home without her," Aaron smirked as he mimicked the well-known commercial.

"I'm ignoring you," Angela huffed as she marched defiantly out to the car.

Angela's prayer: *Dear God, I didn't really want to stay home by myself. But I didn't want to go just because I had to. Does that make sense? Amen.*

4

Angela sat slumped in the pew at church, a bit of space separating her from her family, and watched Aaron perform his "little angel" routine. He even went up for the children's sermon, which Angela knew he thought he was too old for.

Great! I hope he learned something, Angela thought as she watched her younger brother march back down the aisle with the rest of the kids.

Angela slid further over in the pew, hoping no one would make the connection between Aaron and her. *People should have the right to choose their families*, Angela said to herself, continuing her personal gripe session.

"Psst!" Aaron whispered loud enough to be heard over the music. "Page 443," he announced, handing her a hymn book.

"Leave me alone!" Angela hissed back, beginning to feel a bit conspicuous slumped in the pew while everyone else joined in.

Mr. Wang handed his book to Aaron, who put it back in the rack and began to straighten the cards and envelopes surrounding it.

Funny he doesn't dust for fingerprints, Angela glowered, feeling more and more angry and alone.

A firm hand gripped her shoulder and Angela turned to see her dad sitting next to her. "Mind if I join you?" he whispered, smiling kindly as he sat between Aaron and Angela.

Angela felt her body tighten as she realized her dad was not going to move back across the pew. *Why can't they just leave me alone? Why can't*—Angela's anger was interrupted by a squeeze of her hand.

"You can stay here if you want. I'm just glad you came with us," her dad whispered again and slid back over to Mrs. Wang and Aaron.

All the ugly, mad, angry tightness that Angela had been collecting over the past few days suddenly settled in her throat. She felt like she couldn't breathe. Part of her wanted to hug her dad and part of her wanted to push them all away. She had wanted to feel independent and on her own. Sitting at the end of the pew, watching the rest of her family join in the singing, Angela just felt left out and alone. She needed her family and she hoped they still needed her.

All the people stood for the final verse and Angela quickly slid over and grabbed the songbook before Aaron could get it. Mrs. Wang looked over and gave a startled smile as Angela joined in the singing. Angela smiled too. It felt good to be back in the family. She wasn't really ready to leave. At least, not yet.

Angela's prayer: Dear God, sometimes I feel like two different people. I feel so in-between. Not really grown-up and not just a kid anymore. It's confusing. Sometimes it makes me feel mad. Thanks for people who hang in there with me. Amen.

Action idea: Find someone who needs a family and help them feel like part of yours.

98

"I have summoned you by name, you are mine.
You are precious and honored in my sight.
—Isaiah 43:1,4

•

"I like the way you spit."
—Jason

Just Ask Jason

1

"It will be a unique experience for you," Mrs. Corazon explained enthusiastically to her summer English students.

The class broke up into small bits of conversation as Mrs. Corazon handed out the guidelines for the assignment.

"This is impossible!" Scott spoke up.

"Not to say embarrassing!" Marci broke in. She read from the assignment: " 'Find out your positive characteristics by interviewing five people who have known you two years or more and write a character sketch based on your own personality.' Mrs. Corazon, we're only in eighth grade!"

Mrs. Corazon smiled brightly. "You want your characters to be real. You're supposed to write about

what you know. So write about yourselves. It couldn't be easier."

The class groaned in disagreement as they collected their belongings.

"I'll see you in three days," Mrs. Corazon yelled over the din. "Papers in hand!"

Scott and Marci dodged the crowd by taking the back staircase out to the side alley.

"Who you going to ask?" Marci questioned as soon as they were outside.

"Well, my mom and dad for sure," Scott began. "They think I'm perfect!"

"Little do they know," Marci mouthed off. Scott and Marci were as close friends as a boy and girl could get before people started making a thing about it.

"I see." Scott pretended to be huffed as he dramatically crossed Marci's name off his list of potential interviewers.

Marci held her books tightly over her heart and threw her hand over her forehead. "Crushed, I'm sure. Besides, you've only known me since fifth grade. That's one year too short."

"Or two years too many," Scott said, "depending how you look at it."

"OK! OK! You win," Marci laughed. "But besides your parents, who still likes you?"

"Well, there's Sam, the guy down at the bike shop," Scott offered.

"You're going to ask Sam what he thinks about you?" Marci was dumbstruck.

"Ah . . . I see what you mean. It does sound a little strange. Hey Sam! What do you like about me the most?" Scott struck Sam's name from the list. "This is not going to be easy."

"Well, I'm not going to think about it until I get something to eat," Marci yelled, running past Scott toward the Hamburger Hut two blocks from school.

"I'm broke," Scott called after her.

"I'm buying," Marci motioned him to follow. "It's probably the only way I'll get anyone to say anything nice about me."

"That's not true," Scott said a few minutes later as they slid into a booth.

"What's not true?" Marci replied, studying the menu.

"That the only way you'll get someone to tell you something good about yourself is to pay them. There are lots of nice things about you," Scott added.

"Name one!" Marci laughed off the compliment.

"No, really," Scott insisted. "You're always putting yourself down. Or haven't you noticed?"

"Oh, lighten up," Marci said, trying to evade Scott's question. "Let's order, OK?"

Marci managed to swallow a hamburger with a side order of hush puppies and flirt with the cute waiter at the same time. The waiter remained unimpressed, even when Marci attempted to interview him for her assignment.

"They have to know you two years, not two minutes," Scott scolded as he dragged Marci from the restaurant.

"Give me a break! I'm desperate. . . . Do you think I could interview myself? I could make myself sound pretty good," Marci said, testing the idea on Scott.

Scott shrugged and headed off across the street. "Let me know what you find out!" he yelled back as the light started flashing.

Marci smiled until Scott was clearly out of sight. Alone, her face darkened. "Let's see. Counting Mom, that only leaves four people left. Four people who know me and still like me. Four people who probably don't even exist," Marci mumbled, jumping over a pile of Legos, one roller skate, and two Big Wheels before she entered her front door.

Marci's prayer: Dear God, if there is anybody out there who knows the real me and still likes me, please let me know. Amen.

2

"Marci's home!" five little voices yelled before Marci could even get her foot in the door.

"Hi, Mom," Marci yelled over the crowd of little people who were hugging her knees.

Marci's mom provided licensed day-care in her home. Five was the least amount of kids she usually had.

Marci counted heads. "Where's Luke and Lindsay today?" she asked her mom.

"Chicken pox. The whole family. It will probably go right through the kids," she said, pointing to the crew pulling books and papers from Marci's pack. "Think you could take these guys outside for an hour? I'm swamped today."

Marci knew her mom worked hard at her job. "Kids are important," she was always saying. Sometimes Marci wished she was still a little kid so she could get some of the attention from her mom, too. There just wasn't enough "mom" to go around.

"Scoot!" Marci ordered to the band gathered by the backdoor. "Underdogs for anyone who wants!"

Squeals and shouts filled the backyard as Marci pushed each child on the swings at least a thousand times.

"I'm bushed," she finally said, collapsing into the sandbox.

Brian and Leesie fought for room on her lap.

"You're fun!" Brian shouted two inches from her face.

"Funny, funny!" added Leesie, choosing from her two-year-old vocabulary.

"Yeah," Marci chortled, "Funny looking!"

"Oh, no," Brianna, Brian's older sister, said quite seriously. "You're beautiful, Marci."

"Thank you, darling," Marci joked, batting her eyelashes.

Not to be outdone, Jason joined in. "And you give great underdogs, too. Better than my dad!"

"And hugs, too!" Benji finally chipped in.

"Whoa!" Marci held up her hands. "Slow down, I've got to get my notebook."

Three minutes later, Marci sat completing her assignment with the help of five preschoolers.

"Let me see if I got this right," Marci checked. "So you think I'm a funny, beautiful—"

"Beau-u-u-utiful," Brianna repeated.

"Thank you, Brianna," Marci said, pulling the little girl into her lap. "Let's see: a funny, beau-u-u-tiful, huggy person who gives good pushes. Is that what you like about me the best?" Marci asked as five pairs of eyes stared seriously at the paper.

"I like the way you spit," Jason added, not wanting to be outdone.

"Thank you, Jason," Marci laughed, "but I think I'll leave that one off the list!"

Who's That in My Mirror?

Marci's prayer: *Dear God, did you tell those little kids what to say? Amen. P.S. Mrs. Corazon loved my paper.*

Action idea: Next time you can't think of anything good to say about yourself, go and ask a little kid. They almost always tell the truth.